GHOSTS
AND
HAUNTINGS

GHOSTS
AND
HAUNTINGS

M.R.YOUNG

FROM THE AUTHOR
Thank you for purchasing Ghosts And Hauntings: True
Stories of Horror from around the world.

I truly hope you enjoy the stories in this book.
The stories in this book are not fiction and every attempt was made
to ensure all information is accurate to the best of our abilities.

COPYRIGHT
Ghosts And Hauntings by M. R. Young
www.mryoungbooks.com
© 2019 M. R. YOUNG

CONTENTS

CHAPTER 1

SLOSS FURNACES

Sloss Furnaces is a National Historic Landmark in Birmingham, Alabama in the United States. It operated as a crude iron-producing blast furnace from 1882 to 1971. After closing, it became one of the first industrial sites (and the only blast furnace) in the U.S. to be preserved and restored for public use. In 1981, the furnaces were designated a National Historic Landmark by the United States Department of the Interior. The circumstances that lead to it's closing can only be described as supernatural. The source of the phenomenon seemingly coming from the death of a foreman, James "Slag" Wormwood.

Wormwood was foreman of the "Graveyard Shift", the period between sunset and sunrise, where a crew of nearly 150 workers toiled to keep the furnace fed. During the summer months, temperatures throughout the plant would reach more than 120 degrees. Between the lack of sleep, the heat, and low visibility, working the furnace was considered a living hell, literally. Only the poorest of workers, desperate for employment, would work it. These workers, mostly recently arrived immigrants and slave workers, were forced to live in cramped housing located on the furnace site. Where they could be forced, at any moment, to return to work.

In order to impress his supervisors, Wormwood would make his workers take dangerous risks, forcing them to increase the speed of production to unmanageable rates. During his time as foreman,

47 workers lost their lives, ten times more than any other shift in the history of the furnace. Countless other workers lost their ability to work due to accidents and mishaps. There was even a recorded explosion in a small engine house in 1888 that left 6 workers burned and blind. There were no breaks, there were no holidays, there was only the furnace and the mountains of coal needed to keep it going.

In October of 1906, James Wormwood's time as foreman was cut short. It is said that he lost his footing at the top of the highest blast furnace and plummeted into a pool of molten iron ore. His body was instantly melted. It was reported that Woodward must have become dizzy from the methane gas created by the furnace and lost his balance, even though he had never set foot on top of the furnace during his years of employment. Many believe that the workers had finally had enough of Wormwood's sadistic management and fed him into the furnace. No workers were ever brought to trial despite the rumors. Sloss Industries discontinued the graveyard shift soon after his death, citing numerous reports of accidents and "strange incidents" that decreased steel production.

That is when the haunting of Sloss Furnaces began. Workers complained of an "unnatural presence" they encountered throughout the work site. A night watchman in 1926 sustained injuries after being pushed from behind and told by an angry deep voice "to get back to work." The man, upon searching the grounds, could find no sign of any other living person.

In 1947, three supervisors mysteriously went missing. They were found, unconscious, and locked in the small boiler room in the southeastern part of the plant. None of the three men could explain exactly what happened to them. All agreed they were approached by a man whose skin appeared badly burned, who angrily shouted at them "to push some steel."

Probably the most terrifying tale occurred in 1971. The night before the plant closed, Samuel Blumenthal, the Sloss Night Watchman, was taking a last look about. Soon he found himself face to face with "the most frightening thing he had ever seen". He described it as "evil", a "half man/half demon" who tried to push him up the stairs. When Blumenthal refused, the monster began to beat him with its fists. Upon examination by a doctor, Blumenthal found he was covered with intense burns.

There have been more than 100 reports of suspected paranormal activity at Sloss Furnaces recorded in Birmingham Police records. From minor incidents such as steam whistles apparently blowing by themselves, to major sightings and the rare physical assault. It is interesting to note that the majority of these reports happen in the months of September and October at night, during the old "graveyard shift."

There have been numerous investigations of the furnaces. In 1988, a study was conducted by the Center for Paranormal Events (CPE) in St. Petersburg, Florida on Sloss Furnaces. While no events out of the ordinary occurred during the study (which occurred in May), many of the team members claimed that due to the "violent disregard for and loss of life" Sloss Furnaces should be considered "a location rife with restless souls."

The next investigation was in the year 2000, Sloss was studied by the paranormal team of Fox's Scariest Places who concluded that it was one of the highest rates of unnatural energy they had encountered. In early 2002, a skeptical investigative team from CBS Affiliate WJTV investigated the site. They left the furnaces convinced that Sloss was haunted, capturing amazing footage that can been seen on their site.

Another investigation was held in 2003 by the Alabama Foundation for Paranormal Research that have been quoted as saying, "There is no doubt Sloss is a hot spot for paranormal activity. During our investigations, we pulled data that confirms, through our scientific methods and approach, that energies are present that cannot be explained. Sloss is one of the most paranormal places our team has investigated.".

On October 4 of 2003, another assault happened. Josh Thomas, who had worked at Sloss for many years, suddenly caught fire. He claimed to see a strange shape before the fire started. He suffered burns up and down his body and was taken to the hospital. Strangely enough, this was almost on the exact 32nd anniversary of the Samuel Blumenthal burn attack.

In 2005, two psychic investigators from the TV show AIRLINE! investigated Sloss Furnaces. In the middle of the taping, one of them began to spontaneously bleed from a cut that appeared in his right hand, halting the investigation. The camera crew managed to catch images of spirits on their cameras before the investigation ended.

Unexplained Mystery investigation team investigated Sloss in 2009. They captured shadows on film. Ghost Adventures visited and were physically assaulted again, caught on film. In 2014, TAPS (Ghost Hunters) visited Sloss Furnace and filmed 'absolutely phenomenal' footage proving that there is definitive spiritual activity at Sloss and have since returned to capture even more evidence.

Sloss is currently used to hold metal arts classes and events, food festivals, fun runs, educational programs, weddings, and concerts. Sloss Furnaces holds Historic Night Tours to give visitors a chance to hear the darker history of Sloss. For many years Sloss Furnaces has been used as a haunted house attraction during the Halloween season. The event is termed "Fright Furnace at the Historic Sloss Furnaces".

Wormwood's death seems to be the start of the supernatural occurrences. His spirit seems to hang around the furnaces still enforcing his insane work ethic on anyone caught on the site during his shift. He seems to have invited some friends to help him enforce his rules. Or maybe he is the demonic spirit people have encountered. Sloss Furnaces is an old place with lots of tragedy in it's past. Between a slave driving foreman, not existent safety rules, and dangerous conditions the site has plenty of spirits calling it home. Careful when you visit you might get burned.

CHAPTER 2

———◆———◆———

THE ELLIS HOTEL

As humans we tend to think that we can beat the odds, or worse we think we can take on nature. This hubris has lead to countless deaths. The Ellis hotel is one such venture that has caused deaths. It is called the "Titanic of Georgia" because of the misfortune experienced at the hotel. Much like the Titanic. The only thing to blame was our own hubris.

The Ellis Hotel (then the Winecoff Hotel) opened in 1913 as one of the tallest buildings in Atlanta. The steel-framed structure was built on a small lot measuring 62.75 feet by 70 feet, bounded by Peachtree Street, Ellis Street and an alley, with 4,386 square feet per floor. Guest rooms extended from the third to the fifteenth floors, with fifteen rooms on a typical floor. Corridors on guest floors were arranged in an H-shape, with two elevators and the upward flights of stairs opening into the cross halls, and opposing downward runs of stairs converging on a single landing from the legs of the H. The single stairway, of non-combustible construction, was not enclosed with fire-resistant doors. While the use of multiple stairways was becoming common practice in tall buildings, the Atlanta Building Code of 1911 permitted buildings on lots of less than 5,000 square feet to have a single stairway. The steel structure was protected by structural clay tile and concrete fireproofing.

The hotel was touted in advertisements and on its stationery as "absolutely fireproof".

Interior partitions, including the walls between corridors and guest rooms were hollow clay tile covered with plaster. Room doors were 1.5-inch (3.8 cm) wood, with movable transom panels above each door for ventilation between the rooms and corridors, closed by a wood panel of less than .5 inches (1.3 cm) in thickness. The corridor walls were finished with painted burlap fabric extending up to wainscot height. Guest rooms were finished with as many as seven layers of wallpaper. The hotel had a central fire alarm system, manually operated from the front desk, and a standpipe with hose racks at each floor. There was no automatic sprinkler system. The Ellis was within two blocks of two Atlanta Fire Rescue Department engine and two ladder companies, one of which was within thirty seconds of the hotel.

On December 7th, 1946 a massive fire broke out at the hotel. The fire's point of origin was on the third floor west hallway, where a mattress and chair had been temporarily placed in the corridor, close to the stairway to the fourth floor. One theory suggests that a dropped cigarette may have ignited the mattress or other combustibles in the corridor. The fire was first noticed about 3:15 a.m. by a bellboy who had gone to the fifth floor to help a guest and was trapped. However, the first (and only) call to the fire department was made at 3:42 a.m. by the night manager, who was reported to have attempted to warn guests by telephone of the fire. The building fire alarm was not sounded, although by that time no escape was possible from the upper floors in any case. A survivor recounted being awakened and made aware of the fire by the sound of people screaming.

The first engine and ladder companies arrived within thirty seconds of the call. By that time people were already jumping from windows. Fire department ladders could extend only part way up the building, but many guests were rescued in this manner. Other people were rescued via ladders placed horizontally across the alley to an adjoining building.

Fire spread was initially hampered by the stair arrangement. While the stairs were not closed off by doors, the configuration placed ascending and descending runs around the corner from each other, keeping fire and hot gas from quickly ascending the stairs.

Fire did not spread through the enclosed elevator shafts, nor through the laundry or mail chutes. Open transoms between the rooms and the corridors admitted fresh air for combustion, eventually creating a flue-like effect with the fire climbing to all but the two top floors. Once established in the corridors, the fire fed on the burlap wall coverings and ignited room doors and transoms. Doors and transoms were burned through on all but the fourteenth and fifteenth floors. Guests opened windows seeking fresh air and rescue, further enabling the draft of fresh air to the fire. The fire investigation revealed that an open transom was closely associated with the ignition of a given guest room and its contents.

Firefighters were hampered, and in some cases injured by falling bodies. A number of guests tied bed sheets together and tried to descend. Others misjudged the ten-foot-wide alley between the rear of the Ellis and the Mortgage Guaranty Building and attempted to jump across. The Atlanta Fire Department mustered 385 firefighters, 22 engine companies and 11 ladder trucks, four of which were aerial ladder units, at the scene. A second alarm was sounded at 3:44 a.m. and a third at 3:49 a.m., with a general alarm (all available units respond, including off-duty personnel) at 4:02a.m. Mutual aid from surrounding departments brought a total of 49 pieces of equipment. Firefighters climbed adjoining buildings to fight the fire and rescue guests, including the 12-story Mortgage Guaranty building across the 10-foot (3 m) wide alley, and the six-story Davison-Paxon department store (later Macy's) on the opposite side of Ellis Street.

Of the 304 guests in the hotel that night, 119 died, about 65 were injured and about 120 were rescued uninjured. The hotel's original owners, the Winecoffs, who lived in an apartment in the hotel, died in the apartment. Thirty-two deaths were among those who jumped, or who fell while trying to descend ropes made of sheets tied together to reach the ground or too short fire ladders. Among the hotel guests were forty high school students on a State YMCA of Georgia ("Y" Clubs) sponsored trip to Atlanta for a state youth-in-government legislative program, thirty of whom died. The students had mostly been placed two to a room at the back of the hotel next to the alley, where many of the windows had been covered by louvered shutters for privacy. The occupants of the shuttered rooms were killed on every floor above the fifth floor.

The paranormal activities experienced today seem to echo the events of that massive fire. Crying and screaming can be heard. The faint scent of smoke is reported from time to time. Another common occurrence is for the hotel's fire alarm to be triggered at 2.48am – the exact time that the blaze broke out in 1946. Various apparitions can be seen around the hotel. Workers at the hotel claim that tools go missing. The sound of footsteps is also reported. The most unsettling of the activity is the faces that appear in the windows. The faces seem to be contorted in terror.

The hotel is still up and running. Many visitors flock to the hotel because of its reputation of being haunted. Though the hotel has tried to move away from it's haunted image, it doesn't deny it's dark history. So if you decide to stay, make sure you watch for faces in the windows and keep an ear out for the sounds of those caught in the fire.

CHAPTER 3

THE GREENBRIER GHOST

Many people wish they could speak to loved ones after they've passed. Especially, when their loved ones died of mysterious reasons or were killed by an unknown assailant. What if a person could come back to tell us what happened to them? How would that change how we handled murders? Well in the case of the death of Elva Zona Heaster, not much changed.

Elva Zona Heaster was born in Greenbrier County sometime around 1873. Almost nothing is known of her early life, other than that she was brought up near Richlands and that she gave birth to a child out of wedlock in 1895. In October 1896, Zona met a drifter named Erasmus Stribbling Trout Shue; he had moved to Greenbrier County in search of a new life, and to work as a blacksmith. Erasmus found work in the shop of one James Crookshanks; Zona met him not long after his arrival in town. The two fell in love and soon married, despite objection to the match by Zona's mother, Mary Jane Heaster, who had taken an instant dislike to Erasmus. The couple lived together happily for a short time.

Unfortunately, on January 23rd of 1897, Zona was found dead. Her body was discovered by a young boy who had been sent to the house by Erasmus. Her body was found at the bottom of the stairs, stretched out with her feet together and a hand on her stomach. The boy ran home and told his mother, who summoned the local doctor and coroner, George W. Knapp. It took Dr. Knapp almost an hour to arrive at the home.

When the doctor arrived, Erasmus had already carried his wife upstairs and laid her out on the bed. He dressed the corpse himself, which at that time was unusual as traditionally the women of the community washed and prepared the body for burial. Erasmus had dressed her in a high-necked dress with a stiff collar and placed a veil over her face. Erasmus remained by his wife's body as Dr. Knapp examined her. He cradled his wife's head and cried. Not wanting to worsen Erasmus' grief, Dr. Knapp gave the body a very brief examination. He noted some bruising on her neck, but when he tried to look closer Erasmus reacted so violently that the doctor ended the examination and left the house. Zona's death was initially listed as "everlasting faint", but was later changed to "childbirth".

Dr. Knapp had been treating her for "female trouble" for two weeks before her death. It is unknown whether or not she was in fact pregnant. Zona's parents were soon informed of her death. Mary Jane Heaster is reported to have said "the devil has killed her" upon hearing the news of her daughter's death. Zona was buried January 24th in the local cemetery called the Soule Chapel Methodist Cemetery. Erasmus kept a vigil at the head of the open coffin during the move. The wake was held in the Heaster's house. Erasmus behavior soon began to arouse suspicion. His grief repeatedly swung between overwhelming sadness and "incredible energy" He didn't allow anyone close to the coffin, especially as he placed a pillow on one side of her head and a rolled up sheet on the other. He claimed that he was trying to help his wife "rest easier". Erasmus also tied a large scarf around Zona's neck claiming that "it was her favorite", tearfully.

As the body was moved to the cemetery, several people noticed a "strange looseness" to Zona's head. Mary Jane was convinced that her son-in-law had murdered her daughter. After the wake, she removed the sheet from inside the coffin and tried to return it to him. He refused to take it. Mary Jane noticed that the sheet had an odd smell to it and decided to wash it. The water in the wash basin turned red as she dropped the sheet in. The sheet turned pink and the water cleared. The stain would not come out of the sheet and Mary Jane took it as a sign that her daughter had been murdered. She began to pray . She prayed every night for 4 weeks, hoping that Zona would return and tell her what had become of her.

According to local legend, Zona appeared to her mother in a dream four weeks after the funeral. She said that Erasmus was a cruel man who abused her, and who had attacked her in a fit of rage when he believed that she had cooked no meat for dinner. He broke her neck; to prove this, the ghost turned her head around until it was facing backwards.

Supposedly, the ghost appeared first as bright light, gradually taking form and filling the room with a chill. She is said to have visited Mrs. Heaster over the course of four nights.

Armed with the story allegedly told to her by the ghost, Mary Jane Heaster visited the local prosecutor, John Alfred Preston, and spent several hours in his office convincing him to reopen the matter of her daughter's death. Whether he believed her story of the ghost is unknown, but he did have enough doubt to dispatch deputies to re-interview several people of interest in the case, including Dr. Knapp. He was likely responding to public sentiment, as numerous locals had begun to suggest that Zona had been murdered. Preston himself went to speak to Dr. Knapp, who stated that he had not made a complete examination of the body, due in part to how Erasmus had reacted. This was viewed as sufficient justification for an autopsy, and an exhumation was ordered and an inquest jury formed.

Zona's body was examined on February 22, 1897 in the local one-room schoolhouse. Erasmus had vehemently complained about this turn of events, but was required by law to be present at the autopsy. He said that he knew he would be arrested, but that no one would be able to prove his guilt.

The autopsy lasted three days, and found that Zona's neck had indeed been broken. According to the report, published on March 9, 1897, "the discovery was made that the neck was broken and the windpipe mashed. On the throat were the marks of fingers indicating that she had been choked. The neck was dislocated between the first and second vertebrae. The ligaments were torn and ruptured. The windpipe had been crushed at a point in front of the neck." On the strength of this evidence, and his behavior at the inquest, Erasmus was arrested and charged with the murder of his wife.

Erasmus was held in the jail in Lewisburg while waiting for the trial to begin. During this time, more information about his past began coming to light. He had been married twice before. His first marriage ended in divorce, with his wife accusing him of great cruelty. His second wife died under mysterious circumstances less than a year after they were married. Zona was his third wife, and Erasmus began talking about his wish to marry seven women. He spoke openly of this ambition while in jail, and told reporters that he was sure he would be let free because there was so little evidence against him.

The trial began on June 22, 1897, and Mary Jane Heaster was Preston's star witness. He confined his questioning to the known facts of the case, not mentioning her ghostly sighting of her daughter. Erasmus' lawyer questioned Mrs. Heaster extensively about her daughter's visits on cross-examination, perhaps hoping to prove her an unreliable witness. The tactic backfired when Mrs. Heaster would not back down or waver in her account despite the intense badgering. As the defense had introduced the issue, the judge found it difficult to instruct the jury to disregard the story of the ghost. Many people in the community seemed to believe it.

Erasmus was found guilty of murder on July 11 and sentenced to life in prison. However, according to reports accessed, the Greenbrier ghost was never mentioned by the prosecution and played no part in the case against Erasmus. A lynch mob was formed to take him from the jail and hang him, but the mob was disbanded by the deputy sheriff before any damage was done. Four of the mob's organizers later faced charges for their actions.

Erasmus was moved to the West Virginia State Penitentiary in Moundsville, where he lived for three more years. He died on March 13, 1900, the victim of an unknown epidemic, and was buried in an unmarked grave in the local cemetery. Mrs. Heaster never recanted her story of her daughter's ghost, and died in September 1916. As for Zona, her ghost was never seen in the area again.

If only it were as simple as asking the deceased who killed them. Murderers everywhere would think twice about taking a victim, if they could come back and point them out. There would be no chance of getting away with it. Maybe we should all just keep in mind that if someone kills us, we can always come back like Zona did and put them behind bars.

CHAPTER 4

———— ❖ ————

BONAVENTURE CEMETERY

Cemeteries are where everyone eventually ends up. Most cemeteries are quiet places to mourn the death of loved ones. Some cemeteries however are full of life, despite being a resting place for the dead. Bonaventure Cemetery is one of the livelier cemeteries. Most people believe in the stories that come out of the cemetery, others believe it to be nothing more than the imaginations of visitors that cause these stories. The only way to find out for certain is to visit the cemetery yourself.

Whether Bonaventure Cemetery is haunted or not, it can certainly lay claim to being a famous cemetery. It is the grand final resting place of Jim Morrison and Oscar Wilde along with songwriter Johnny Mercer, novelist Conrad Aiken, numerous town dignitaries, and veterans from the American Revolution and Civil War. Bonaventure Cemetery is also famous for its beauty. Placed beside the Wilmington River, some claim this view was the inspiration for Mercer's Moon River. The atmospheric cemetery is a sculpture garden of towering obelisks, detailed crypts covered in ivy, intricate headstones carved with poetic epitaphs, and strikingly realistic statues. The cemetery is a tranquil park of pink azaleas and roses, and avenues of Savannah's live oaks, draped with swaying tendrils of Spanish Moss. The grounds are teeming with birds and butterflies.

Bonaventure Cemetery stands on the grounds of a former plantation originally owned by John Mullryne. According to local legends, the main house caught fire sometime during the late 1700s. Inconveniently, the blaze occurred during a dinner party. The host thought the party was far too good to end there, so they took it outside. The servants carried the table and chairs after them, and the dinner party continued by the light of the raging fire. The host graciously continues to entertain his guests who raise their glasses to him, the house, and the glowing fire. The Host made a toast in which hoped that the party would never end and at the conclusion of the toast he dramatically smashes his crystal glass against an oak tree. The guests follow suit. This event echoes across time. Tradition has it that if you listen closely on quiet nights you can still hear the laughter and the shattering of crystal glasses.

The Cemetery is inhabited by an abundance of angel and cherub statues. According to folklore, some of these statues are also haunted, such as the angel that reportedly changes facial expressions. People believe her countenance transforms from showing anguish, sorrow, to peacefulness. Bonaventure is also populated by statues of its inhabitants. According to reports, these lifelike monuments come to life; babies cry, children play, and Corinne, a beautiful young woman, smiles. Corrine smiling is said to be a wonderful thing, as she took her own life.

The most infamous ghost of Bonaventure Cemetery is Little Gracie. In her perpetual pose, the little girl with chubby cheeks and sharply-cut bangs sits beside a tree trunk, clutching a flower. She wears a high neck frilly collar, a buttoned sailor dress and spat boots. A plaque by her grave shares her story. Little Gracie Watson was born in 1883, the only child of her parents. Her father was manager of the Pulaski House, one of Savannah's leading hotels, where the beautiful and charming little girl was a favorite with the guests. Two days before Easter, in April 1889, Gracie died of pneumonia at the age of six. In 1890, when a rising sculptor named John Walz, moved to Savannah, he carved from this life-sized, delicately detailed marble statue from a photograph, which for almost a century has captured the interest of all passersby. Perhaps it is because her statue bears such an uncanny resemblance to her, or because it is tragic that she died at such a tender age, that some like to believe Little Gracie still lives.

Visitors leave toys for her ghost to play with, and claim she cries tears of blood if her playthings are removed. There is always a collection of toys near her tomb, especially around Christmas time. There's a belief that if you place a quarter in Gracie's hand and encircle her statue three times, the coin will disappear. With her down-turned marble hands, nothing can be placed on her palms, but her tomb is still a wishing well of coins. The grave has been fenced off because visitors would also rub the statue for good luck.

Another little girl calls this cemetery her home. Little Wendy, also known as the "Bird Girl", wears a long dress and a contemplative expression; her head tilted to the left as she holds a bowl in each outstretched hand. The statue is haunted by the ghost of Lorraine Greenman, the little girl who posed for the artist, Sylvia Shaw Judson. Little Wendy once stood sentinel over the Trosdal family plot, but she is so idolized that the owners donated the statue to Savannah's Telfair Museum of Art to avoid her destruction.

People also seem to hear dogs in the cemetery. For some it's normal barking, others hear growling and snarling. There have been reports of people being attacked by these ghostly hounds. Others have simply been chased off the property. Though the strangest part of Bonaventure's history isn't the ghost that make the cemetery their home, but the living legend that lived nearby.

Minerva the Voodoo Queen as she was called in the mystery novel Midnight in the Garden of Good and Evil. Her real name being Valerie Fennel Aiken Boles. She was a voodoo practitioner that lived near the cemetery was said to use the soil from the cemetery in her rituals. She was thrust into the public eye after the book was turned into a movie. She didn't like all the attention and absolutely didn't like for people to touch her or take her picture. She claimed that doing so would open her up to hexes. She died in May of 2009.

Bonaventure Cemetery is a beautiful place, rich with history. The ghostly inhabitants seem to enjoy it there. The cemetery itself lies in a residential area and the residents find it absolutely charming. People often take walks and enjoy picnics in the cemetery. The Bonaventure Cemetery is a wonderful example of humans and spirits living in harmony.

CHAPTER 5

THE BELL WITCH

Imagine being tormented by something you can't see. Something that taunts you and your family with disembodied voices. It takes your health from you and seems obsessed with ending your life. That was the life of a man in the 1800's named John Bell. John Bell moved his family from North Carolina to the Red River bottom land in Robertson County, Tennessee, settling in a community, Red River, which became Adams, Tennessee many years later. Bell purchased some land and a large house for his family. Over the next several years, he acquired more land, increasing his holdings to 328 acres, and cleared a number of fields for planting.

The haunting began after John Bell, as he was out inspecting his corn field, stumbled upon a strange creature. The creature was described as having the body of a dog and the head of a rabbit. John fired a shot at the creature and it disappeared. John's son, Drew, spoke of seeing a bird of extraordinary size and Betsy, John's youngest daughter, claimed to see a girl in a green dress swinging from the limb of an oak tree. Soon the family began hearing knocking along the outside walls and doors of their home. The frequency and force of the knocks increasing every night. Soon after that the children started experiencing terrifying incidents. The children were having their covers ripped off of them and their pillows thrown to the floor. They were also hearing what sounded like rats gnawing on their bed posts. They then started having their hair pulled and were being scratched. Betsy got the worst of it, though. She was slapped, pinched and stuck with pins, often leaving welts and hand prints on her face and body.

Soon the family began to hear whispering voices. They were too soft to be understood, but sounded like and old woman singing hymns. The entity's voice strengthened over time to the point that it was loud and unmistakable. It sang hymns, quoted scripture, carried on intelligent conversation, and once even quoted, word-for-word, two sermons that were preached at the same time on the same day, thirteen miles apart. The entity also gossiped about other families in the settlement. Telling the Bell family of things that went on in other homes. The entity claimed at one point to be "Old Kate Batts' witch" and was called Kate from that point forward. John Bell Jr. often had conversations with the "witch" and she seemed to develop a level of respect for him.

The Bell family weren't the only people to experience the witch's haunting. John, at one point, sought out the help of his friend, James Johnston. James and his wife came and spent the night at the Bell house and were subjected to the same happenings as the children. As word of the haunting spread, people came from all over to experience it for themselves. John Johnston, one of James' sons, devised a test for the witch. He asked something no one outside his family would know, what his Dutch step-grandmother in North Carolina would say to the slaves if she thought they did something wrong. The witch replied with his grandmother's accent, "Hut tut, what has happened now?". An Englishman stopped to visit and offered to investigate. After commenting on his family overseas, the witch suddenly began to mimic his English parents. Early morning the next morning, the witch woke him with the voices of his parents. The Englishman quickly left that morning and later wrote to the Bell family. He told them that the entity had visited his family in England. The had been awoken by his voice while he was at the Bell house. He apologized for his skepticism.

Word of this supernatural phenomenon soon spread outside the settlement, even to Nashville, where then-Major General Andrew Jackson took a keen interest. John's three eldest sons had fought under General Jackson in the battle of New Orleans. Jackson decided to visit the Bell farm and see what all the buzz was about. Jackson's entourage consisted of several men, some horses, and a wagon. As they approached the Bell property, the wagon stopped suddenly. The horses couldn't pull it.

After several minutes of cursing and trying to coax the horses into pulling the wagon, Jackson proclaimed, "By the eternal, boys! That must be the Bell Witch!". Then, a disembodied female voice told Jackson that they could proceed and that she would see them again later that evening. They were then able to proceed across the property, up the lane, and the Bell home where Jackson and John Bell had a long discussion about the Indians and other topics while Jackson's entourage waited to see if the entity was going to manifest.

One of the men claimed to be a "witch tamer". After several uneventful hours, he pulled out a shiny pistol and proclaimed that its silver bullet would kill any evil spirit that it came into contact with. He went on to say that the reason nothing had happened to them was because whatever had been disturbing the Bells was "scared" of his silver bullet.

Immediately, the man screamed and began jerking his body in different directions, complaining that he was being stuck with pins and beaten severely. A strong, swift kick to the man's posterior region, from an invisible foot, sent him out the front door. Angry, the entity them spoke up and announced that there was yet another "fraud" in Jackson's party, and that he would be identified and tormented the following evening. Now terrified, Jackson's men begged to leave the Bell farm. But Jackson, on the other hand, insisted on staying so that he could ascertain who the other "fraud" was. The men eventually went outside to sleep in their tents, but continued begging Jackson to leave. What happened next is not clear, but Jackson and his entourage were spotted in nearby Springfield early the next morning.

Over time, Betsy Bell became interested in Joshua Gardner, a young man who lived not far from her. With the blessing of their parents, they decided to marry. Almost everyone was happy about their engagement. The entity, for reasons unknown to this day, repeatedly told Betsy not to marry Joshua Gardner. Betsy and Joshua could not go to the river, the field, or the cave to play without the entity taunting them persistently. Their patience finally reached its limit, and on Easter Monday of 1821, Betsy met Joshua at the river and broke off their engagement. The disturbances decreased after Betsy ended the engagement, but the entity continued to express its dislike for John Bell and vowed relentlessly to kill him.

At times, the spirit displayed a form of kindness, especially towards Lucy, John Bell's wife. Often calling her "the most perfect woman to walk to earth". The witch would give Lucy fresh fruit and sing hymns to her. John on the other hand seemed to be wasting away. Bell had been experiencing episodes of twitching in his face and difficulty swallowing for almost a year, and the illness seemed to grow worse with time. By the fall of 1820, his declining health had confined him to the house, where the entity began removing his shoes when he tried to walk and slapping his face when he experienced seizures. Her loud, shrill voice could be heard all over the farm, cursing and chastising "Old Jack Bell," as she often referred to him. John Bell breathed his last breath on the morning of December 20, 1820, after slipping into a coma the day before. Immediately after his death, the family found a small vial of unidentified liquid in the cupboard. John Bell, Jr. gave some of it to the cat, which died instantly. The entity then spoke up, exclaiming joyfully, "I gave Ol' Jack a big dose of that last night, which fixed him!". John, Jr. quickly threw the vial into the fireplace, where it burst into a bright, bluish flame and shot up the chimney.

John Bell's funeral was one of the largest ever held in Robertson County, Tennessee. As family and friends began leaving the graveyard, the entity laughed loudly and began singing a song about a bottle of brandy. It is said that her singing didn't stop until the very last person left the graveyard. The entity's presence was almost nonexistent after John Bell's demise, as if its purpose had been fulfilled. In April of 1821, the entity visited John Bell's widow, Lucy, and told her that it would return for a visit in seven years. The entity returned in 1828, as promised. Most of its visit centered around John Bell, Jr., with whom the entity discussed such things as the origin of life, civilizations, Christianity, and the need for a mass spiritual reawakening. Of particular significance were its nearly accurate predictions of the Civil War and other events.

The witch left again after three weeks, but vowed to visit John Bell's most direct descendant in 107 years. The year would have been 1935, and the closest living direct descendants of John Bell at that time was Nashville physician, Dr. Charles Bailey Bell. Dr. Bell himself wrote a book about the "Bell Witch," published in 1934. No follow-up was published, and Dr. Bell died in 1945.

CHAPTER 6

◆———————————◆———————————◆

BLOODY MARY

Urban legends are becoming the modern version of folk tales. Every place has their own version of the story unique to them. Some are so wide spread that they are known internationally. Some even taking on new aspects of the culture they've now become a part of. Most are presented as fact, and maybe some are.

One notable urban legend is that of "Bloody Mary". Bloody Mary is a legend consisting of a ghost, phantom, or spirit conjured to reveal the future. She is said to appear in a mirror when her name is chanted repeatedly. The Bloody Mary apparition may be benign or malevolent, depending on historic variations of the legend. Bloody Mary appearances are mostly "witnessed" in group participation play.

The story as to who "Bloody Mary" is is often the main change from place to place. The ritual itself started as a way to see the future. The ritual encouraged young women to walk up a flight of stairs backward holding a candle and a hand mirror, in a darkened house. As they gazed into the mirror, they were supposed to be able to catch a view of their future husband's face. There was, however, a chance that they would see a skull (or the face of the Grim Reaper) instead, indicating that they were going to die before they would have the chance to marry.

In the ritual of today, Bloody Mary allegedly appears to individuals or groups who ritualistically invoke her name in an act of catoptromancy (or divination using a mirror). This is done by repeatedly chanting her name into a mirror placed in a dimly-lit or candle-lit room. In some traditions the name must be repeated thirteen times (or some other specified number of times). The Bloody Mary apparition allegedly appears as a corpse, witch or ghost, can be friendly or evil, and is sometimes "seen" covered in blood. The lore surrounding the ritual states that participants may endure the apparition screaming at them, cursing them, strangling them, stealing their soul, drinking their blood, or scratching their eyes out.

There are two main ideas as to who "Bloody Mary" is. The first being Mary Worth. Mary Worth was a witch who, according to local tradition, lived on the Old Wagon Road in Chicago during the Civil War. It is said that she used to kidnap runaway slaves and keep them chained in her barn, doing who knows what to them in her dark rituals. The locals eventually became furious enough to take the law into their own hands and burn Worth at the stake. The legend says her body was buried in St. Patrick's Cemetery. Doubtful, since an infamous witch would have never been laid to rest in a Christian cemetery. Instead, she may have been buried on her farm, as one couple learned the hard way.

Many decades after Mary Worth's execution, a farmer and his wife bought her former property and, fully aware of the place's history, built their home on the very foundations of the barn in which Worth practiced her black arts. Apparently not one to be scared by old legends, the farmer set out to clear the land for an oat field. During his work, he came across a square stone and moved it to the door of the house, figuring it to be a good stepping stone. This proved to be a mistake. Violent and often dangerous events immediately began to plague the couple, with the wife finding herself locked in the barn or the house on multiple occasions and plates crashing on the floor by themselves. As the activity worsened, the farmer began to wonder if he had inadvertently disturbed Mary Worth's real grave site. He tried to return the stone to its original place in an attempt to end the disturbing phenomena, but he never could find the exact spot. After several years of torment, the house burned to the ground in 1986, supposedly due to arson.

The second identity is of a young mother whose name was Mary. Mary had two children, whom she loved dearly. One day as the children were out playing they disappeared. According to which story the children were either killed or just lost. Some even believe they were the victims of a serial killer. She waited for them to come home for months but they never returned. Struck with grief, Mary smashed her face into the bathroom mirror repeatedly until she passed out and died from blood loss. This is why she haunts mirrors and appears to be covered in blood.

In this legend to conjure her, you look into the mirror and say three times, "Bloody Mary, I have your children". She is said to appear in the mirror looking frantic, searching for her lost children. You have to leave the room before she discovers that you lied or she will scream and try to attack you. She will claw at your chest trying to rip out your heart, like hers was ripped out by the loss of her children. Though, in some stories, she may come and speak with you if instead of saying you have her children you say that you are sorry about her children. She will appear to you still covered in blood but instead she will be crying. You can ask her a yes or no question, she will answer by nodding or shaking her head. She will then fade from the mirror. Some other variations of the story has "Mary" as a babysitter who lost a child and was killed over it. Another version has "Mary" as a demon who appears as a woman to gain sympathy and your trust, so that it may invade your home and take over your body.

Some people also believe that "Bloody Mary" comes from a more historical place. They believe that it stems from the story of Mary I or Mary Tudor. Mary was the queen of England and Ireland from July 1553 until her death. She is best known for her aggressive attempt to reverse the English Reformation, which had begun during the reign of her father, Henry VIII. The executions that marked her pursuit of the restoration of Roman Catholicism in England and Ireland led to her denunciation as "Bloody Mary" by her Protestant opponents. She is said to have burned 280 people at the stake. How she connects to the "Bloody Mary" is vague, but many people believe she appears out of hatred of being called "Bloody Mary".

There are even similar stories under different names around the world. Hanako-San from Japan is a great example. According to legend, Hanako-san is the spirit of a young girl who haunts school bathrooms. The details of her physical appearance vary across different sources, but she is commonly described as having a bobbed haircut and as wearing a red skirt or dress. The details of Hanako-san's origins also vary depending on the account; in some versions, Hanako-san was a child who was murdered by a stranger or an abusive parent in a school bathroom. In other versions, she was a girl who committed suicide in a school bathroom. Other versions state she was a child who lived during World War II and who was killed in an air raid while hiding in a school bathroom during a game of hide-and-seek.

To summon Hanako-san, it is often said that individuals must enter a girls' bathroom (usually on the third floor of a school), knock three times on the third stall, and ask if Hanako-san is present. If Hanako-san is there, she will reply with some variation of "Yes, I am." Depending on the story, the individual may then witness the appearance of a bloody or ghostly hand. The hand or Hanako-san herself is said to pull the individual into the toilet, which may lead to Hell or the individual may be eaten by a three-headed lizard.

Regardless of what story you believe, people all over the world believe there is a spirit haunting the world's mirrors. Who is to say they are wrong? People for centuries have been seeing strange things in mirrors. In most cultures mirrors are used to confuse spirits. Some people even believe that a mirror can trap a spirit and that is why they cover the mirrors in the home of someone who has died. Many diviners use mirrors to speak to those who have died. Mirrors are often seen as portals to other realms or planes.

Maybe "Bloody Mary" is just a silly game kids play at sleepovers. Maybe it is based on a true story? Just be wary, legends always contain some variation of the truth. One day you may find yourself looking into the mirror and seeing something other than your reflection. You may find yourself stuck staring into the eyes of something not quite human. Hopefully it will be friendly, hopefully it will leave.

CHAPTER 7

─────◆─────◆─────◆─────

CECIL HOTEL

Hotels are known for being places where people come and go often. People rarely stay at a hotel longer that a couple weeks. Yet despite this fact, many hotels are host to spirits. Most believe this is due to the prevalence of violence and death that seems to surround certain hotels. No hotel knows this better than the Cecil Hotel. At least 16 different murders, suicides, and unexplained paranormal events have taken place at the hotel and it's even served as the temporary home of some of America's most notorious serial killers.

The Cecil was built in 1924 by hotelier William Banks Hanner. It was supposed to be a destination hotel for international businessmen and social elites. Hanner spent $1 million ($15 million today) on the 700-room Beaux Arts-style hotel. It flaunted a marble lobby, stained-glass windows, palm trees, and an opulent staircase. Hanner would come to regret his investment. Just two years after the Cecil Hotel opened, the world was thrown into the Great Depression. Los Angeles was not immune to the economic collapse. The area surrounding the Cecil Hotel would eventually be dubbed "Skid Row" and become home to thousands of homeless people. The once beautiful hotel soon gained a reputation as a meeting place for junkies, runaways, and criminals. Worse yet, the Cecil Hotel ultimately earned a reputation for violence and death.

The Cecil hotel had six reported suicides in the 1930's alone. The methods of suicide included ingesting poison, slitting their throats, and jumping out of windows. On November 19, 1931, Manhattan Beach resident W. K. Norton, 46, was found dead in his room after ingesting poison capsules. A week prior, Norton had checked into the Cecil under the name "James Willys" from Chicago. Norton's death appears to be the earliest known suicide at the hotel. In September 1932, a maid found Benjamin Dodich, 25, dead from a self-inflicted gunshot wound to the head. He did not leave a suicide note.

In late July 1934, former Army Medical Corps Sgt. Louis D. Borden, 53, was found dead in his room at the Cecil. He had slashed his throat with a razor. Borden left several notes, one of which cited poor health as the reason for his suicide.

In March 1937, Grace E. Magro fell from a ninth story window. Her fall was broken by telephone wires which were wrapped around her body. She later died at the now-demolished Georgia Street Receiving Hospital. Police were unable to determine whether Magro's death was the result of an accident or suicide.

In January 1938, United States Marine Corps fireman Roy Thompson, 35, jumped from Cecil's top floor and was found on the skylight of a neighboring building. He had been staying at the Cecil for several weeks. In May 1939, Navy officer Erwin C. Neblett, 39, was found dead in his room after ingesting poison.

The next few decades only saw more violent deaths. In September 1944, 19-year-old Dorothy Jean Purcell awoke in the middle of the night with stomach pains while she was staying at the Cecil with Ben Levine, 38. She went to the bathroom so as not to disturb a sleeping Levine, and, to her complete shock, gave birth to a baby boy. She had no idea she had been pregnant. Mistakenly thinking her newborn was dead, Purcell threw her live baby out the window and onto the roof of the building next door.

The next strange death was in 1962. 65-year-old George Giannini was walking by the Cecil when he was struck to death by a falling woman. Pauline Otton, 27, jumped from her ninth-floor window after an argument with her estranged husband. Her fall killed both her and Giannini instantaneously.

While tragic calamities and suicide have contributed heavily to the hotel's body count, the Cecil Hotel has also served as a temporary home for some of the grisliest murderers in American history.

In the mid-1980s, Richard Ramirez, murderer of 13 people and better known as the "Night Stalker" — lived in a room on the top floor of the hotel during much of his horrific killing spree.

After killing someone, he would throw his bloody clothes into the Cecil's dumpster and saunter into the hotel lobby either completely naked or only in his underwear. Which went mostly unnoticed since "the Cecil in the 1980s was total, unmitigated chaos" according to reporters at the time. At the time, Ramirez was able to stay there for a mere $14 per night. And with corpses of junkies reportedly often found in the alleys near the hotel and sometimes even in the hallways, Ramirez's blood-soaked lifestyle surely went unnoticed at the Cecil.

In 1991, Austrian serial killer Jack Unterweger, who strangled prostitutes with their own bras, also called the hotel home It is believed he chose the Cecil hotel for it's connection to Richard Ramirez. The area around the Cecil Hotel was popular with prostitutes, Unterweger's prime victims. Unterweger stalked these types of areas time and time again searching for his next victim. One prostitute he is believed to have killed vanished right down the street from the hotel. Unterweger even claimed to have "dated" the hotel's receptionist.

Some murders connected with the Cecil remain unsolved. One of the most notable, being the case of the "Black Dahlia". The victim, Elizabeth Short, was reportedly staying at the Cecil before her death. What connection her death may have had to the Cecil is not known, but what is known is that she was found on a street not far away on the morning of January 15 with her mouth carved ear to ear and her body cut in two.

Another unsolved murder was the murder of "Pigeon Goldie" Osgood. Osgood was well known around the area and had earned her nickname because she fed birds in nearby Pershing Square. Near her body was the Los Angeles Dodgers cap she always wore and a paper sack full of birdseed. Osgood was found by a hotel worker. She had been raped, stabbed and beaten. A suspect was found in a park nearby. He was wearing bloodied clothes. He was cleared of the crime however and her case remains unsolved to this day.

Unfortunately, these tales of violence aren't limited to the past. In 2013, a college student named Elisa Lam was found dead in the water tank of the hotel. Her naked body was only discovered after guests started complaining of bad water pressure and a "funny taste" to the water. Before her death, surveillance cameras caught Lam acting strangely in an elevator, at times appearing to yell at someone out of view, as well as apparently attempting to hide from someone while pressing multiple elevator buttons and waving her arms erratically. The security video footage of the last moments of her life can be found online. The last body found in the hotel was of a man who committed suicide in 2015.

Paranormal activity has been reported all over the hotel. People report being touched. Whispers can be heard throughout the hotel. There have been several reports of people getting "lost" in the hotel. Often finding themselves on the wrong floor, with no idea how they got there. The batteries of electronic devices seem to drain almost instantaneously. Some people claim to have their hair pulled and blankets pulled off in the middle of the night.

With so many deaths at this place one might begin to wonder if the hotel is cursed. Many people believe that the spirits inhabiting the hotel are causing some of the misfortune that befalls the guests that stay here. Many people are inclined to believe that theory. While others just chalk the misfortunes up to the area around the hotel being as bad as it was.

The hotel's grisly history was the inspiration for the popular television show, American Horror Story: Hotel. Many recent visitors have reported that the staff have been acting extremely strangely concerning filming in the hotel. One such individual stating that security was called on him by a member of the staff as he wandered around the halls. This has caused many people to believe they are trying to cover up the dark history of the building. Which, considering the hotel is now under renovation to turn it into a micro-apartment complex, isn't much of a stretch. Regardless of whether or not you believe the Cecil Hotel is haunted, one thing is for certain. The building has seen far too much violence and death.

CHAPTER 8

•————•————•

AMITYVILLE HOUSE

Home is where most people feel the safest. It's where you can be yourself and relax Not every house is a home, though. Some houses are anything but safe. Some are host to things that will stop at nothing to bring suffering and death upon the occupants. Unfortunately, some of the harmful entities get their wish. Such is the case of the Amityville Horror House.

On November 13, 1974, in the small town of Amityville, New York, Ronald Defeo burst into Harry's Bar and screaming that his parents had been shot and killed. Police went to investigate and discovered the bodies of the Defeo family; The father, mother and 4 of the 5 Defeo children were found, face down, shot in the back of their heads. Ronald claimed he wasn't home during the murders, and had only discovered the bodies of his parents prior to arriving at Harry's Bar. After police officers found a gun case for a .35 caliber Marlin Rifle in Ronald's Room, however, he confessed.

Ronald and his lawyer tried to enter a plea of insanity during trial. The insanity plea was supported by the psychiatrist for the defense, Daniel Schwartz. The psychiatrist for the prosecution, Dr. Harold Zolan, maintained that although Defeo was a user of heroin and LSD, he had antisocial personality disorder and was aware of his actions at the time of the crime. After the extremely long trial Ronald Defeo was found guilty of the murders. He was sentenced to six consecutive life sentences.

Though the case is considered solved, there never has been a solid explanation of how one person acting alone could take the lives of six family members in the dead of night and no one heard the shots being fired. Ronald Defeo has offered several different recountings of events over the years, none of them seem to hold water.

On December 18, 1975, the Lutz family moved into the Defeo home, only been 13 months since the Defeo murders had occurred, George and Kathleen Lutz thought the Dutch colonial was a lovely home and a steal at $80,000. They never expected they'd have to leave it all behind 28 days later. A catholic priest arrived while the Lutz family was unpacking to bless the family home. The priest made his way upstairs to the second floor. He entered the bedroom which had formerly belonged to Marc and John Defeo. He began sprinkling holy water at which point an unseen voice told the priest to get out, which he hastily did.

The Priest did not tell the Lutz family about the voice, but he did warn them not to use the upstairs room as a bedroom and not to let anyone sleep there. The Lutz family abided by the words of the priest and turned the room into a sewing room. From the very first night they moved in, the family claimed they felt strange feelings. Within days the family's personality had drastically changed and arguments ensued.

George was plagued by a chill that never seemed to leave and spent all his time feeding the fire place. George and Kathy's health declined drastically. The Lutz's daughter, Missy, began spending all her time in her room playing with an imaginary friend. She described the imaginary friend as a red eyed pig called Jodie. Jodie could transform not only shape but size, at times being larger than the house. Jodie also claimed she could not be seen by anyone unless she wanted them to.

In the early morning hours of Christmas Day 1975, George looked up at the house after checking on the boathouse and saw "Jodie" standing behind Missy at her bedroom window. When he ran up to her room he found her fast asleep with her small rocking chair slowly rocking back and forth. Missy would also sing constantly while in her room. Whenever she left the room she would stop singing and upon returning she would resume singing where she left off. Kathy had vivid nightmares about the murders and discovered the order in which they occurred and the rooms where they took place. The Lutz children also began sleeping on their stomachs, in the same way that the dead bodies in the Defeo murders had been found.

The house also started having strange problems. Mysterious odors, ranging from perfume to excrement, would emanate from different locations of the house where no wind drafts or piping would explain the source. Black stains appeared on the toilets and ceramic fixtures and a green gelatin substance would appear throughout the house. Locks on the doors and windows were all damaged by an unseen force. Hundreds of flies appeared in the sewing room despite it being the dead of winter. George discovered a small hidden room (around four feet by five feet) behind shelving in the basement. The walls were painted red and the room did not appear in the blueprints of the house. The room came to be known as "The Red Room". This room had a profound effect on their dog, Harry, who refused to go near it and cowered as if sensing something ominous.

George would wake up nightly at 3:15 am which coincided with the time the police felt the Defoe's were murdered. George also awoke one night to witness his wife transform into a 90-year-old woman with shocking white hair, her face a mass of wrinkles and ugly lines, and saliva dripping from the toothless mouth. The next night, Kathy received red welts on her chest caused by an unseen force and was levitated two feet in the air as she layed in bed. The Lutz family tried on numerous occasions to contact the Catholic priest only to find the phones would cut out or produce static whenever they would try to call. After failing to get the priest to return, the family took matters into their own hands. Armed with a crucifix, they walked throughout the house reciting the Lord's Prayer. A chorus of voices erupted in response, asking them, "Will you stop?"

The final night was reported to be the worst, banging and wrappings as loud as a marching bands emanated throughout the house, furniture being moved by its own accord, and the children being terrorized. After 28 days in the Defeo home, the family claimed they could take no more. They grabbed only a few belongings and fled the house, taking shelter at Kathy Lutz's mother's home in nearby Babylon. Twenty days after the Lutz's fled, Paranormal Investigators Ed & Lorraine Warren were called in by Marvin Scott, a news reporter with channel 5 NY, who had covered the Amityville story and worked on a prior investigation with the Warrens. A team of reporters, investigators, and parapsychologist were assembled by Ed Warren and met at the home at 112 Ocean Avenue, the Lutz family refused to re-enter the home during the investigation.

During the investigation Ed was physically pushed to the floor while using some religious provocation in the basement. Lorraine was also overwhelmed by a Demonic presence and was plagued by psychic impressions of the Defeo Families bodies laid along the floor covered in white sheets. Lorraine was also physically pushed. The research team also captured an image of spirit that appeared as a little boy peering from the second floor.

The land was also found to be used by John Ketchum . John Ketchum was a practicing black magician and had a cottage on the land prior to the construction of the Dutch Colonial house in 1924. John requested that his remains be buried on that property. Along with whatever John brought on to the property, The Shinicock Indians also at one time had an enclosure on this land. It was used to house the sick and the mad, those in this enclosure were left to die. The Warrens believed that the suffering there had left the property with a very negative energy and dark history. Such a negative history was a magnet for demonic spirits and the preternatural. The Warrens believe these energies directly impacted the lives of both the Defoe's and the Lutz's. The Warrens retrieved a handful of the Lutz's possessions and deed for the property. The Lutz's sold the rest of their belongings and relocated to California.

The Ocean Avenue home is again on the market. While there have been no further reports of activity from recent residents, it leaves one to wonder if the malevolent spirits are lying in wait. Maybe they have left after the house being vacant for so long. No one can know for certain. Thought it does present the question, was Ronald Defeo acting of his own accord or was he being controlled by forces beyond our comprehension? Or maybe him spilling blood is what invited the entities in? There are many unknowns in the Defeo case and the house has certainly left an imprint on the Lutz's. The only thing we know for certain is that something untoward happened in that house and it has become a dark spot in the history of Amityville, New York.

CHAPTER 9

❖────•────•─────❖

TERESITA BASA

There have been films and books made about people returning from the grave to give their loved one messages. Most revolve around the idea that they are trying to help their family deal with their sudden deaths and even helping to shed light on what happened. We are fascinated with the idea of spirits coming back to help solve their murders. That is why when it happens in real life, The news is spread far and wide and is very seldom forgotten easily.

Teresita Basa was born in the Philippines in 1929 and lived a very privileged life; she was the sole child of a very successful lawyer and his wife. After graduating from Assumption College in Manila, Basa came to the United States where she received a master's degree in music from Indiana University and then went on to study inhalation therapy. Eventually, Basa settled down in Chicago, Illinois, where she became a respiratory therapist at Edgewater Hospital. She was known to be a very reserved and polite woman who was exceptionally dedicated to her job where she took pride in providing the best care for her patients. As well as being hardworking in her career, Basa also attended Loyola University where she was preparing a doctor's thesis on music. She spent what little free time she gave piano lessons and started writing her very own book. She wasn't a drinker and led a very routine and quiet life.

At around 7:30PM on the 21st of February, 1977, Ruth Loeb, a friend from the hospital, telephoned Basa. The duo chatted for almost half an hour; Basa mentioned she had a male guest coming over but never identified him. Almost an hour later, two neighbors of Basa smelt smoke. They informed the janitor, who alerted the other residents and then phoned the fire department. On that crisp cold evening in February of 1977, the shrill sound of a fire engine could be heard speeding towards the apartment block on N. Pine Grove Avenue. As they extinguished the fire in apartment number 15b they were more than horrified to find a nude body hidden under a smoldering mattress. They were even more shocked to discover that the body had a butcher knife embedded in the middle of the chest. The body was soon identified as Teresita Basa. To all appearances, it was a rape-murder, with Basa's clothing folded beside her nude body. However, a medical examination determined that Basa had not been raped.

Detective Joseph Stachula and his partner, Lee R. Epplen were assigned to the case. Over the forthcoming weeks, they interviewed friends and acquaintances of Basa, so they could determine what kind of a person she was. In the burnt apartment, they discovered a mysterious note written by Basa which read: "Get tickets for A.S." They were unfruitful in uncovering who A.S. could have been and eventually, the case rolled to a standstill. However, in August, police in Evanston contacted Detective Stachula and queried him about an Allan Showery, a technician Edgewater Hospital. Evanston police referred Detective Stachula to Dr. Juan Chua and it was here, that this case takes a very peculiar turn.

Dr. Juan Chua was a surgical assistant at Franklin Boulevard Community Hospital and according to him, his wife, Mrs. Remy Chua, was possessed by Teresita Basa. He explained to the stunned officers that his wife had sporadically gone into a comatose state and would speak in the voice of another woman. At one point during these trances, Mrs. Chua blurted out: "I am Teresita Basa." Afterwards, while speaking in Tagalog, Mrs. Chua claimed that she had been stabbed to death by Allan Showery. Dr. Chua said he asked the voice why she had admitted Showery to her home, to which she replied because "he was a friend." When Mrs. Chua snapped out of the trance around half an hour later, she had no recollection of what she had just said to her husband. Initially, Dr. Chua and Mrs. Chua were apprehensive about contacting police out of fear "we would only appear foolish". However, when the voice of Basa returned several times, they finally decided they would contact police.

Police initially weren't convinced; Mrs. Chua was a Philippine native herself and had briefly worked at the same hospital as Basa and Showery. While Mrs. Chua had met Basa during an orientation session, the two worked different shifts. However, when Dr. Chua told police that the voice of Basa had claimed that Showery had also stolen jewelry from her apartment; this was something that even the police didn't know about. According to the voice of Basa, Showery had given some of the jewelry to his common-law-wife. After getting Showery's address, Detective Stachula and Detective Epplen went to his apartment on the 11th of August. Showery confessed that he knew Basa but denied ever visiting her apartment. Shortly afterwards, he changed his story and claimed he had gone to her apartment to fix her TV but claimed he had left immediately afterwards. While at the apartment, the two detectives noticed that Showery's common-law-wife, Yanka Kamluk, was wearing a pearl cocktail ring which was eerily similar to the one described as stolen by the voice of Basa. They soon discovered other pieces of jewelry which would be identified as belonging to Basa by her family.

After presented with this evidence, Showery confessed to the murder of Basa. In his confession, he declared that he had gone to Basa's apartment to rob her so that he could pay his rent. He said that all he got was $30 and a handful of jewelry. Showery would later claim that he was "just kidding" when he made the confession. During his trial, prosecutor Thomas Organ roared "Well, Allan Showery, you weren't kidding when you plunged the knife into Teresita Basa's chest!" During Showery's trial, his defense lawyer, William Swano, suggested that Mrs. Chua faked the trances because she had been fired from the hospital. The first trial was declared a mistrial when the jury met a deadlock. A new hearing was scheduled for February of 1979.

Meanwhile in his jail cell, Showery seemingly had a change of heart and decided to plead guilty to the murder of Basa as well as robbery and arson. Many whispers speculated that the spirit of Basa visited Showery in his cell. More likely, however, his defense lawyers suggested he change his plea to receive a more lenient sentence and receive a lenient sentence he certainly did. Showery was sentenced to 14 years in prison for the murder and concurrent terms of 4 to 12 years on the armed robbery and arson charges. Showery was paroled from Stateville Correctional Center in July of 1983, after serving just under five years. "To this day, I'm not quite sure whether I believe how the information was obtained," said Detective Stachula. "Nonetheless, everything is completely true."

Over the forthcoming years, many sleuths have tried to explain these seemingly paranormal trances. Some have suggested that Showery had complained about Mrs. Chua's work quality thus leading to her being fired from the hospital. In fact, her psychic symptoms allegedly started shortly after her termination. Could she have heard Showery speaking about his involvement in the murder? Whether or not one believes the claims that Mrs. Remy Chua was possessed by the spirit of Teresita Basa, the clues given led to the arrest and conviction of her killer.

To this day, the murder and ensuing mystery is arguably one of the most bizarre murder cases in Chicago history. No one can ever know for certain if Teresita returned from the grave to help convict her killer. Maybe there is hope for other cases that have gone cold. Maybe more people will be believed when they tell others that their loved ones came back and told them who killed them. Either way we know that a killer was put behind bars and Teresita can now rest easy.

CHAPTER 10

—◆———————————◆—

LAKE LANIER

Lake Lanier is the cursed lake of Georgia. Lying in the northern part of the U.S. state of Georgia, sprawled out among the foothills of the North Georgia Mountains for 26 miles, 75 meters (258 feet) deep at its deepest point and with an area of 150 km2 (59 square miles) of water and 1,114 km (692 miles) of shoreline, is Lake Sidney Lanier, commonly referred to as simply Lake Lanier. Actually a man made reservoir, Lake Lanier is the largest lake in Georgia and even sports a chain of islands that were originally large hills before the lake was formed.

The origins of Lake Lanier can be traced back to 1948, when the U.S. government purchased a 100-acre farm from a river ferry operator by the name of Henry Shadburn in order to start a water project on the Chattahoochee River for the purpose of providing the city of Atlanta with hydroelectricity, flood control and water supply. In 1950, the U.S. Army Corps of Engineers began breaking ground and constructing the Buford Dam on the Chattahoochee River, which would be completed in 1956 and begin the process of flooding the foothills to create the lake.

The creation of Lake Lanier was beset with problems from the beginning. Funding for the project faced numerous hurdles which stopped and started construction to the point where it is amazing it was actually finished on schedule. Additionally, the Corps of Engineers, as well as the states which use the Apalachicola-Chattahoochee-

Flint River Basin and the Alabama-Coosa-Tallapoosa River Basin, comprised of Florida, Georgia, and Alabama, all squabble over water flow requirements, consumption caps, how the water should be used, and whether to give it priority as a water supply, hydroelectricity source, or even recreation, all of this while juggling the federal laws that demanded water be set aside for threatened or endangered species that lived in or around Chattahoochee River. The states of Alabama and Florida were particularly unhappy about how the U.S. Army Corps of Engineers regulated the flow of water from Lake Lanier to their states. There was even debate over what the lake should be called, with the builders finally settling on the name of the poet Sidney Lanier.

Then there was the rather destructive nature of the lake's creation. The U.S. government began a mad dash to ravenously purchase land from private companies, farmers, and anyone else who lived in the area that would inevitably wind up underwater. During the 5 years it took for the lake to completely fill to its intended water level, the government would buy up over 50,000 acres of prime farmland and pristine wilderness, moving more than 250 families, 15 businesses, and even relocating 20 cemeteries along with their corpses in the process.

As the nooks and crannies of the mountain foothills filled with surging water, the inexorable spread of the lake devoured entire towns along with their buildings and houses, farmland, fields, bridges, toll gates, historical landmarks, river ferry businesses, a racetrack called Looper Speedway, country roads, forests, and other lakes. Many of the structures that would be inundated were simply left as is, so that if one were to walk along the lake's bottom one would find submerged towns complete with roads, walls, and houses all eerily intact; abandoned underwater ghost towns inhabited only by fish and perhaps ghosts of the past. Even the ferries that were put out of business by the lake's creation were simply abandoned to become rusting hulks littering the bottom and the shore.

This rather eerie history and the spooky presence of whole underwater ghost towns, derelict ghost ships, and desecrated cemeteries, are far from the only strange things about Lake Lanier, and indeed it has accrued a rather sinister reputation for drawing death and suffering to itself.

Over the years, there have been an inordinate amount of deaths associated with the lake, ranging from boating accidents, drownings, and even a fair number of drivers who have lost control of their vehicles to go careening off of roads to crash into the water. There are various stories of boats hitting something in the water only for it to turn out there was nothing there, boats or other watercraft capsizing for no apparent reason, and sudden, dangerous rogue waves that seem to come from nowhere without warning to maraud across the surface. Many of the drowning cases are somewhat odd in that they have happened very close to shore with strong swimmers and in calm conditions, which considering the history of the lake have given rise to rumors that Lake Lanier is somehow haunted or cursed.

Some who have almost drowned here and lived to tell the tale have told of feeling as if they were being pulled underwater or held under by unseen hands, or of having the air suddenly seem to leave their lungs and cause exhaustion with startling suddenness. In some of the cases, people who drowned fairly close to shore have had their bodies turn up in positions far from where they died, which is probably due to currents but when mixed with spooky rumors becomes a case of ghostly forces dragging corpses through the water before discarding them.

In 2011, this menacing reputation for accidents and deaths began to get more public attention when there were a total of 17 deaths on Lake Lanier, many due to freak accidents. In 2012 the trend continued when a quick succession of violent deaths and horrific injuries occurred here which made national news. The first of this wave of deaths happened on June 18, 2012, when 9-year-old Jake Prince and his brother Griffin, 13, were riding a pontoon out on the lake and were struck and killed by a speeding boat driven by a Johns Creek business owner named Paul J Bennett, 44. Mere weeks after this tragic accident, on July 9, 11-year-old Kile Glover, who happened to be the son of the popular pop star Usher's ex-wife, Tameka Foster, was struck while riding an inner tube by a family acquaintance riding a jet ski and rendered braindead. Although doctors struggled to save his life, he died two weeks later on July 21 and was taken off life support. A 15-year old friend of the boy was also seriously injured in the same incident, but ultimately recovered. These tragic accidents took the media by storm, and before long Lake Lanier was being deemed "cursed" and "a death trap" by the news and social media sites such as Twitter, with many people insisting that it was an evil, vile place that was best avoided.

While these were perhaps the most high profile deaths to occur on Lake Lanier, these sorts of accidents and drownings have been happening with unsettling frequency since the lake was first opened to the public. While a lot of people have been quick to call the lake cursed, one of the more likely reasons for these incidents is probably due to the area's rapid rise as a popular place to visit. Besides being a water source and hydroelectric plant for Atlanta and the surrounding areas, from around 1962, Lake Lanier has become a popular recreational area complete with hotels, full-service boating marinas, restaurants, campgrounds, stables, beaches, a golf course, and even a full water park. People of all ages come here for boating, swimming, fishing, camping, and other outdoor activities, to the tune of around 8 million visitors a year. Adding to the dangers already inherent with so many droves of people converging on the lake, often with a good amount of alcohol involved, there are also very few regulations for operating boats or motorized watercraft and those that are in place are weakly enforced. With so many people driving around in boats and swimming, in many cases under the influence of alcohol, there are bound to be quite a few accidents. Yet nevertheless, there are still those who insist that even considering these circumstances, the number of deaths, weird accidents, and injuries at Lake Lanier is unusually high, and believe the lake is truly cursed, haunted, or both.

In addition to the myriad freak accidents and drownings that seem to constantly plague the area, Lake Lanier has been the location for more bizarre and mysterious deaths and disappearances that still remain unsolved. One such case revolves around a Georgia man by the name of Kelly Nash, 25, who went missing from his home in Buford, Georgia, on January 5, 2015. Early that morning at 4AM, Nash awoke with flu-like symptoms such as coughing and sneezing, and told his girlfriend Jessica Sexton, who was with him at the time, that he felt terrible and should probably see a doctor before going back to bed. Sexton then woke up again at 7:30 AM to find that Nash was gone and had not taken his wallet, car keys or ID with him. When Nash still had not returned that evening, police were called in and it was discovered that a 9mm pistol was missing from the house but none of Nash's other belongings were missing or out of place.

A massive search would subsequently be launched for Nash, involving authorities, family and friends, and dogs specially trained to sniff out dead bodies, and a $50,000 reward was offered for any information, yet no trace of the man or his whereabouts were found. It was not until one month after his strange disappearance, on February 8, that Nash's badly decomposed body was found in Lake Lanier by a fisherman. Nash was still wearing pajama pants and dark shirt that he'd had on when he went missing, and although the body appeared to have no major trauma, it was found that he had suffered a single gunshot wound to the head. The crime has never been solved and it is unclear why he chose to go out in the middle of the night in his sleeping clothes, how he ended up at the lake, and whether he committed suicide, if there was foul play involved, or if the lake's alleged curse had anything to do with it.

In another mysterious case, a 16-year-old Gainesville High School student by the name of Hannah Truelove went missing from an apartment complex near Lake Lanier where she lived with her mother on the morning of Aug. 24, 2012. The following day, Hannah's body was found in a wooded area by the lakeside by another resident of the apartment complex. The girl had been stabbed multiple times, yet it was unclear if the wounds were life threatening and the actual cause of death remained elusive, although authorities were able to rule out drowning. Making the case even creepier was a series of tweets Hannah had made on Twitter shortly before her death that expressed general discontent with her life at the apartment complex and her fear of a stalker, with one chilling tweet allegedly stating "So scared right now." Hannah's father would later claim that his daughter had made no mention of being under any duress and had not seemed any different or more upset than usual in the days leading up to her disappearance and death. Authorities were never able to glean any insights or information from the tweets, and indeed no leads would ever come up and no suspects were ever apprehended in the case, despite a major investigation and exhaustive interviews with neighbors and nearby residents, none of whom had seen or heard anything suspicious on the day in question, as well as continuous pleas for any information pertaining to the case. Hannah Truelove's death remains a mystery.

One of the most notorious deaths associated with Lake Lanier is also the source of one of its alleged ghostly mysteries. In April of 1958, a young woman who worked at Riverside Military Academy, Delia Parker Young, and her friend, Susie Roberts, headed off to Three Gables in Dawsonville in Susie's 1954 Ford for a night out. They would never return. A subsequent investigation into their disappearance discovered that they had visited a gas station that night and left without paying. The only clue left at the scene was a set of skid marks across the road which seemed to suggest that the car had skidded off of Lanier Bridge on Dawsonville Highway and into the lake below, yet no vehicle could be found. Divers who were brought in to search for the car were unable to locate it due to poor visibility in the murky water and the masses of sheared off tree trunks that litter the lake's bottom. For 18 months, police were unable to find any further clues and no trace of the missing women or the car, but then a fisherman named C.A. Simpson made a gruesome discovery when the decomposed body of what was thought to be that of Delia Parker Young suddenly floated up out of the depths. Oddly, the corpse, which could not be completely positively identified at the time, was missing two toes from the left foot and both hands. It was never ascertained just why the body was missing its hands and toes or what the cause of death had been. With no way of knowing if the corpse was that of Delia, it was eventually buried in an unmarked grave in in Alta Vista Cemetery. The body of Susie Roberts and the car remained missing, despite repeated searches.

The mystery would baffle authorities for decades until November of 1990, when construction on an expansion of Lanier Bridge was under way. As construction crews were dredging the bottom of the lake in order to set up pillars for the expansion, they uncovered a rusted out hulk of a 1954 Ford which held within it the remains of a human body. The car had been hidden within tree trunks, mud, and other detritus in 90 feet of water on a steep slope. The body was decomposed to the point of being unidentifiable, but the belongings found on it, including a purse, rings, and watch were able to conclusively prove that the body was that of the long missing Susie Roberts. In light of this discovery, it was concluded that the other body had indeed been Delia Parker Young, the headstone was changed accordingly, and Susie Roberts was buried beside her.

Interestingly, although the deaths of Delia Parker Young and Susie Roberts is an old, mostly forgotten case, it has spawned one of the area's most persistent and frightening local legends. It is said that a ghostly young woman dressed in a blue dress and missing her hands can sometimes be seen walking up and down the length of Lanier Bridge, and is said to be the ghost of Delia Parker Young, since she had been dressed in a blue dress on the night of her death and her body had been found minus hands. According to those who claim to have seen the ghost, which has since become known as The Lady of the Lake, Delia's restless spirit seems to be searching for her missing hands.

The reports of mysterious forces pulling swimmers underwater or causing boats to capsize, and the Lady of the Lake are not the only cases of potentially paranormal happenings on Lake Lanier. There have been occasional reports of a mysterious raft equipped with a lantern on a pole, ridden by a shadowy figure that uses a pole to push it along, and which allegedly appears and disappears out of nowhere. In one particularly harrowing account, two fishermen saw the ghostly raft while out on the lake fishing in a rowboat on one cold autumn night at around 1 AM in the morning. In this case the mysterious raft was around half a mile away and in an estimated 45 feet of water, yet the rider was bizarrely pushing it along with a pole nevertheless. At one point this enigmatic figure shouted something to the two fishermen and proceeded to jump off of the raft into freezing water to swim towards them. This alarmed the two fishermen, who pulled in their lines and were in a hurry to get out of there, thinking it was perhaps someone meaning to do them harm. It was at this point that the lantern on the raft abruptly went out. When the fishermen shone their boat's spotlight out across the water they could find no sign of the raft or the mysterious occupant who had jumped into the water. The black surface of the lake remained calm and the raft would not appear again.

CHAPTER 11

ANNABELLE

Dolls walk a fine line between cute and uncanny, the way their eyes seem to follow you around the room. For many people, dolls are a source of fear. Even to the point of a full blown phobia. The fear of dolls is called pediophobia. For some the mere thought of a doll will send them into a panic attack. The cause of pediophobia isn't understood as of yet. Many theorize that the fears stem from a traumatic event, like watching a horror movie about dolls or an event that is connected to dolls. For some people though, the fear is very much so warranted.

In 1970, a mother purchased an antique Raggedy Ann Doll from a hobby store. The doll had been a birthday present for her daughter, Donna. Donna shared an apartment with a nurse named Angie at the time. Donna loved the doll and kept it displayed on her bed. Within days Donna and Angie started noticing weird occurrences with the doll. The doll seemed to move, even though no one had been in the apartment. It started out small, legs moved or shifted further down the bed. Small enough that the women just brushed it off. Soon though the doll moved into different rooms, The doll would be found with legs crossed, arms folded, other times it would be found upright, standing on its feet. One day Donna left the doll on the couch in the living room and when she came home the doll was sitting on her bed with the bedroom door shut.

A month after the doll had been brought into the apartment Donna and Angie started finding notes, written on parchment. The notes read "Help Us" and "Help Lou" written in a child-like scrawl. Neither woman owned parchment, they had no clue where the parchment was coming from. Lou was a friend of both Donna and Angie. Lou had never been fond of the doll and on several occasions warned Donna that it was evil and to get rid of it. Donna chose to ignore Lou's advice and kept the doll.

One day after work, Donna came home to find the doll had moved onto her bed again. She had grown accustomed to the doll moving about the apartment, but for some reason today felt off. She walked over and inspected the doll. On the doll's hands and chest were drops of a red substance that appeared to be blood. That scared Donna and Angie enough that they sought out the aid of a professional. They called in a medium and a séance. The medium told Donna and Angie that the doll was possessed by the spirit of a girl called Annabelle Higgins. Annabelle was a young girl that resided on the property before the apartments were built. She was only seven years old when her lifeless body was found in the field upon which the apartment complex now stands. The spirit told the medium that she felt comfortable with Angie and Donna and that she wanted to stay with them and be loved. Donna and Angie both felt compassion for Annabelle. Donna gave her permission to inhabit the doll and stay with them. They soon found out however, that Annabelle was not what she appeared to be. She held a darkness they had yet to see.

In the following weeks, the strange occurrences seemed to take a malicious turn. Lou began to have terrible recurring nightmares, almost every single night. One day as he napped in the apartment, he awoke from one of his nightmares to find that he couldn't move. He felt like he was being watched. He looked down to where his feet were. There, standing by his feet, was the doll. He watched as the doll slowly slid up his legs coming to a stop on his chest. The doll began to strangle Lou. Paralyzed and unable to fight back, Lou soon blacked out. He woke the next morning certain that it had not been a dream. Unfortunately, it would not be the last encounter Lou would have with "Annabelle".

Lou and Angie were in Angie's room preparing for a road trip they were leaving for the next day. They were looking over maps, when they began to hear rustling noises coming from Donna's room. They thought that someone had possibly broken into the apartment. Lou determined to figure out who or what it was quietly made his way to the bedroom door. He waited for the noises to stop before entering and turning on the light. The room was empty except for Annabelle whom was tossed on the floor in the corner. Lou scoured the room for forced entry but nothing was out of place. But as he got close to the doll he got the feeling that somebody was behind him. He spun around quickly, but nobody else was there. Then almost instantly, he found himself grabbing for his chest. He doubled over and it felt like he was bleeding. His shirt was stained with blood. He opened his shirt and there on his chest was what looked to be 7 distinct claw marks, three vertical and four horizontal. The marks were hot, like burns. These scratches healed almost immediately, half gone by the next day.

After that encounter, Donna and Angie both knew that this wasn't the spirit of a little girl they were dealing with. Donna contacted Father Hegan, an Episcopal priest. Father Hegan felt he needed to consult someone higher up in the church and contacted Father Cooke. Father Cooke immediately called Ed and Lorraine Warren. The Warrens were American paranormal investigators and authors associated with prominent cases of hauntings. Edward was a World War II United States Navy veteran and former police officer who became a self-taught and self-professed demonologist, author, and lecturer. Lorraine professed to be clairvoyant and a light trance medium who worked closely with her husband. Ed and Lorraine contacted Donna and, after listening to her stories about the doll, concluded that the doll was being manipulated by an inhuman presence. The inhuman presence was looking for a human host to possess. It created the story of Annabelle to play on the heartstrings of Donna and Angie and get their permission to inhabit the home. After the investigation, Ed decided that the apartment needed an exorcism.

Father Cooke performed an exorcism on the apartment. Donna asked that the Warrens take the doll with them to avoid a recurrence. They agreed to take the rag doll back home with them. Upon leaving Ed placed the doll in the back seat. He and Lorraine agreed he would not take the interstate in the event the inhuman spirit still resided with the doll.

His suspicions were proven correct in no time. The Warrens felt themselves the object of a vicious hatred. At each curve the car swerved and stalled, every corner causing the power steering and brakes to fail. Repeatedly the car was on the verge of a collision. Ed reached into the back seat, into his black bag and took out a vial of holy water He doused the doll making the sign of the cross over it. The disturbances stopped immediately and the Warren's arrived safely home. They had hoped that would be the end of Annabelle's malicious behavior. After the Warrens arrived home, Ed sat the doll in a chair next to his desk. The doll levitated a number of times in the beginning, then it seemed to become inactive. In the following weeks, however, it began showing up in various rooms of the house. When the Warrens were away and had the doll locked up in the outer office building, they would often return to find it sitting comfortably upstairs in Ed's easy chair when they opened the main front door.

The doll also showed a hatred for clergymen who came to the house. In one instance Father Jason Bradford, a catholic exorcist, came to the house. Upon seeing the doll seated in the chair he picked it up and said "Your just a rag doll Annabelle, you can't hurt anyone", and tossed the doll back in the chair. Ed warned the young man about antagonizing the doll. Upon leaving an hour later, Lorraine pleaded to the priest to please be careful driving and to call her when he arrived home. A few hours later Father Jason called Lorraine and explained that his brakes failed as he entered a busy intersection. He was involved in a near fatal accident destroying his vehicle.

This would be one of the first accidents that the doll caused.

CONCLUSION

After reading all these ghost stories you're probably a little creeped out. The point of this book isn't necessarily to scare you but to open your mind and to ask yourself... Do ghosts really exist?

Although some extensive research was done for this book and the stories have been validated by first hand sources. Even with all this evidence people will still refuse to believe in the paranormal and may even find it ridiculous. Truth is the universe is full of unexplained phenomena and mysteries that leave us intrigued and asking for answers.

ABOUT THE AUTHOR

M.R. Young was born in 1982 in Sherbrooke, Quebec, Canada and is fluently bilingual in both french and english. He is a strong supporter of animal welfare groups and donates much of his time to local animal rescues. Young currently resides in Calgary, Alberta, Canada with his wife and son.

THANK YOU

Again I'd like to thank you for purchasing this book and I hope you enjoyed reading this collection of stories. There are so many books out there and I really appreciate you picking mine.

If you enjoyed this book, I would like to ask you for a small favor in return. Please take a couple minutes to leave me a review of this book on the retailer web site that you purchased it from. I would really appreciate it! Your feedback will give let me know how much you liked this book, as well as help with improvements for future books.

Printed in Great Britain
by Amazon

10983836R00036